Across the Floors of Silent Seas

A Short Story Prequel to *Till Human Voices Wake Us*

C. S. Johnson

Print ISBN: 978-1-948464-11-6
Ebook ISBN: 978-1-948464-12-3

Dedicated with much love to Sam, as always. I can never quite picture my audience without you present, but I hope my work and the world is better off for it.

Also dedicated with much love and gratitude to Terri, a new friend and fine lady. There are days when I fall into deep waters, but your words have proven to give me the propulsion I need to keep going. God bless you and yours, my sister in Christ.

ACROSS THE FLOORS OF SILENT SEAS

To Get *Awakening* (A Special Christmas Episode of The *Starlight Chronicles*) as a bonus for picking up this book,

Click Here

Or Download It At:

https://www.csjohnson.me/awakening

ACROSS THE FLOORS OF SILENT SEAS

C. S. JOHNSON

3

ACROSS THE FLOORS OF SILENT SEAS

Across the Floors of Silent Seas

***

He knew he was in trouble the second before it happened.

Everything had been going along well for Jay Bishop and his assignment up until that point. He even would've said things were going "swimmingly," if he'd been asked, just to irritate Noelani. His sister was a proud, powerful swimmer who loved to scuba dive as much as he did, but at eight months pregnant, she was stuck up on the research ship with the rest of their classmates.

He could picture Noelani clearly in his mind. Earlier, she had stuck her tongue out at him as his sub launched and disappeared under the waves.

Personally, Jay couldn't blame her for her irritation. As he started to make his way across the ocean floor, slinking his way some sixty feet below sea level, he thought about the dry, data-centric conversations the other doctoral candidates were likely having over their measurements and charts. He knew he had escaped the cold, hard world of facts for one of wonder and discovery.

Awed and grateful, Jay lovingly ran his gloved hands over the ocean floor. It was a mix of rock and sand and other sea fixtures, all gradually heading down into the heart of the world. He watched as small amounts of sea dust shifted at his movements; he smiled, full of childish wonder, as the little twists and spirals reflected back rainbows against the blurry blue darkness.

ACROSS THE FLOORS OF SILENT SEAS

Following the trail of dancing dust, Jay turned his gaze upward toward the surface. He could no longer see the outline of the *Pedro*, even though he knew it was there. Noelani was a pain and a half to deal with, but Jay knew she could steer ships and subs and all sorts of water vehicles as well as he did. Having grown up along the SoCal oceanfront, he liked to think he was one of the best when it came to playing captain.

That's why UC allowed us to take the ship out in the first place. Well, one of the reasons, anyway.

The University of Washington was also talking about setting up an underwater lab, and there was nothing like competition to convince the University of California at San Diego that they needed one, too—and there was nothing like having a batch of grad students and interns around to do the work of mapping out the selected site on the ocean floor.

Which was perfect for him, really; Jay was out along the Middle American Trench, the furthest ends of the Ring of Fire, planting data receptors and taking measurements across the sea floor, all while testing the new super-scuba suit that allowed for deeper diving—*and* getting college credit for it.

Jay loved his work, and if he was given the chance to take over Noelani's diving assignments, that only added to the overall glory. A small laugh escaped him as he began setting up the first data receptor inside a rocky fissure.

"I can hear you and your smugness from here, Jay." Noelani's dry commentary snapped over the radio.

ACROSS THE FLOORS OF SILENT SEAS

"Well, Scripps will be glad their radio tech works even better than expected, then. UC made a good move, buying their prototypes."

"Scripps wants to know about the suit more than wave radio," Noelani reminded him. "Since they commissioned that more recently. And because they allowed an insufferable bone head to take it for a test drive."

"There's no need to be upset at me, Lani," Jay told her. "You'll be diving again in less than two months. Besides, be glad. Both UC and the Institution like having you in command of the mission rather than on it. They seem to like having a woman in charge."

"Only because when I'm underwater now, I'm a liability," Noelani replied dryly.

Jay had to smother another snicker. "Well, we don't want to make the whales jealous, now do we? They gave our last diver some trouble, after all."

As Noelani replied with a string of sailor language at his playful insult to her growing baby belly, Jay tuned her out and headed toward another rocky grove.

But at the thought of whales, he glanced around again. Their other research leader, Kekoa, had been attacked by an orca on their last dive near Juan's fault line.

Jay was just about to ask Noelani about running a sonar scan when he saw a large shadow shift out of the corner of his eye.

"Is something wrong, Jay? Is it Juan?"

ACROSS THE FLOORS OF SILENT SEAS

Jay momentarily forgot the shadow as he heard the sudden worry in Noelani's voice. He did not have to wonder if she was thinking of Kekoa, too.

"It seems he's not as temperamental as you, Lani-my-love." Jay ran his hands, covered with his protective gloves, over the fissure lining on the seafloor. His small amount of diving light was only able to shine a few inches down toward the Juan de Fuca fault line.

"Shut up, Jay."

"That's my girl. No wonder your baby daddy ran off," Jay grumbled. The shadow shifted behind him again; Jay felt the uneasiness of suddenly being alone in the world—and even if it was the world he loved, he felt his patience begin to burn more quickly. Jay shoved another data receptor into the shelf, running the initial diagnostics as he anchored it. He let out a calming breath. *Only a few more to go, and then I'll be able to head back up.*

"Niko didn't run off," Noelani insisted, distracting him again as he kicked his flippered feet toward another rocky ridge. "He got a job promotion, and the company had to move him to New York. He works in the media. It's a great job. He can't just leave it, Jay."

"Sure," Jay muttered.

"Come on, Jay. He said he'll transfer back to San Diego as soon as possible. And he'll be here for the baby when he comes. Niko promised me."

"I'll believe that as soon as the seafloor opens up and mermaids come swimming out," Jay replied with a laugh. "But you believe what you want, darling."

"If you're going to be such a prudist prick about it, I can just leave you here, you know." Noelani bristled. "Don't forget, *Pedro* is one of the faster ships at UCSD. I'll be out of your transmission frequency quicker than you can say 'shark bait.'"

Jay imagined Noelani standing on the bridge of the *Pedro*, angrily fisting her fingers into her long black hair, the hair that was the same shade as his, as she stood by the boat's controls, her big, tanned, pregnant belly pressed up against the console as she prepped for takeoff.

The picture of her in his mind diffused his temper, allowing him to forget all about his feeling of isolation.

"You know you're my whole world, and I love you for it," Jay replied easily enough, pouring on the charm he reserved only for his little sister. In the twenty-six years since she had been born, it had never failed. "Besides, I'm sure you've had worse days with me."

"Shut up," Noelani grumbled, still irritated, but placated. "Just get the reading that Dr. Marley wanted. The rest of the crew is getting annoyed with your meandering as much as your mouth."

"I'm working well enough," Jay argued, trying not to think of Dr. Marley and his high, borderline unrealistic expectations. He appreciated his supervisor, but that only made the thought of disappointing him worse.

"Maybe you're getting to be an old man then," a new voice replied over the radio. "Since you're going so slowly."

Jay smiled as Kekoa came on the line. "I'm younger than you," he reminded him. "You'll be thirty next year. I've still got another six months after that."

"I'm still smarter than you."

"Age has nothing to do with that," Jay said with a laugh.

"I'll say," Noelani said. "I'm smarter and work faster than both of you."

"No you're not," Kekoa insisted, bantering back with her.

"I'm not the one who was chased down by a killer whale, Kekoa."

"He was clearly trying to remedy his inferiority complex," Kekoa replied.

Jay laughed. "You know, if you want to get the data as much as I do, you know we need to do this carefully. Maybe you guys should let me work instead of distracting me with your flirting."

He did not have to see Noelani to know she was rolling her eyes; he was certain of it, just as he was certain Kekoa was blushing.

Jay enjoyed their resulting silence as he spied another optimal spot for a data receptor. He scuttled further down the ocean shelf, tugging some on the line that tied him to his small sub.

The data receptors were monitors with the latest updated software, capable of tracking temperatures and shifts along the ocean floor. With their proximity to the Juan de Fuca Plate and the other tectonic plates, they were essential to any underground construction project.

"If UC wants to build a lab down here," Jay murmured, "I'm going to recommend a movable one."

"Some of the designs they have prepared show that the rooms will be compartmentalized," Noelani said.

"Are the others boring you to death, that you're listening so intently to my remarks, darling?" Jay asked, teasing even though he welcomed her churlish chatter.

"People confuse boredom for stability, and stability for sanity," she muttered.

Jay laughed. "Well, I'm sure some people would never assume we had a solid grip on sanity before we decided to become oceanographers. With several metric tons of water pressure surrounding us at these depths, I'm sure someone would be quick to question our mental facilities and their working order."

"True enough, brother mine." Noelani paused, and Jay knew she was likely rolling her pretty eyes. "And yours especially, since your sanity was barely there to begin with."

"Well, I am sane enough to know a compartmentalized lab is not going to help much if one of those dormant volcanoes decides to wake up," Jay said, pushing the data receptor deep into a crevice.

Everything had been going well, until that moment. And then, in that second, he knew he was in trouble.

The rock he had been pressing against broke, and Jay felt the small rumble ripple out across the sea floor.

Before his imagination could spiral out of control, reality demanded his full attention. A sharp mix of cold and warm water sputtered out from the fissure in front of him, and immediately, Jay screamed. The sheet of rocky shelf underneath him suddenly broke open, plunging him into the dark unknown.

Then, in the twinkling of an eye, Jay felt his world fall into nothingness, as his thick goggles and his scuba gear smothered him, his body choked with pain on all sides. He lost control of his suit, and the pressure pounded into him.

As he struggled along the ocean shelf, he thought he heard Noelani's voice cut through over the radio.

"Jay? Jay!"

Jay grappled against the rocks around him, their sharp edges cutting into his body, while the water pulled him further into the mountain. His breath staggered, and he angrily fought with his mind, fighting to let Lani be the last thing he remembered instead of his fear.

"Lani," he whispered again, watching as the last of his air bubbles whipped away into darkness.

ACROSS THE FLOORS OF SILENT SEAS

He felt himself flounder, and he began praying in silent syllables, begging God, if he was there, to grant him another chance at life.

He was past denial and in the middle of bargaining when the darkness closed in on him, and the earlier shadow from before came rushing toward him.

His hand, no longer covered with the special suit, brushed against something rubbery and smooth.

Jay opened his eyes carefully.

Still fighting for breath, he saw there was a large orca circling around him.

So much for God. And to think Lani was worried about shark bait!

He watched the whale as it circled around once more, watching as the whale picked up speed.

What does it think it's—?

With a resounding crash, the orca's body slammed into the trench walls around him. Jay felt his body tumble free of his rocky prison and slide underneath a shelf of falling rocks.

He felt himself surface, and then his lungs filled up with air …

He was alive. He was alive, and breathing.

Jay whirled around, his body still underwater. He joyfully inhaled a mix of water and air before spitting it out with shock.

"What is this?" he asked, strangely unnerved to hear his voice echo. He looked down at his feet and

ACROSS THE FLOORS OF SILENT SEAS

saw the shadow of an orca swimming out of the corner of his vision.

Instantly, Jay knew where he was—he was in a pressurized air pocket, in a type of small, underground cave.

There were stories of such formations, and Jay had long considered them too rare for him to worry over.

He almost laughed, realizing the irony. He had never worried about drowning before either, although it was a much more likely possibility.

Although now, he thought bitterly, if he wasn't going to drown, he would likely starve to death.

So much for optimism.

ACROSS THE FLOORS OF SILENT SEAS

He reached up and took his goggles off, latching them onto his utility belt.

"Great," he muttered. He shined his light around and realized that the air pocket opened up into a larger room, branching out into a full cave.

He pulled himself over to a larger boulder, and then, after checking to make sure he could stand up to his full height of six feet, headed away from the water. He glanced around the cave as he walked, hoping he would be able to figure out a way to survive until he could be rescued.

"Rescued again," he corrected himself, remembering the orca. *Saved by a Killer Whale*, he thought, amused. He decided if for no other reason, he would have to survive to tell Noelani. And her baby, too.

Jay slumped over against the cave wall, allowing it to provide a rocky cradle of sorts as he allowed himself one full minute of panic.

He had to get out of there if he wanted to see his family.

"It's not like Niko's actually going to be a good father," Jay muttered. He knew Niko was the kind of guy who made promises in the heat of the moment, and then he would walk away the moment he got cold feet.

Which was why when Noelani told Niko the news about their baby, Jay was not surprised at all that Niko "earned" a promotion at work, one that would take him to an office research job in New York City.

ACROSS THE FLOORS OF SILENT SEAS

"Research job, ha." Jay shook his head. He did not have the heart to tell Noelani that research jobs were easily done over the Internet.

He especially did not have the heart to tell Noelani that because he had a feeling she already knew it herself. She was just telling everyone else what she wanted to believe, hoping that if enough people believed her, it would make it true.

Jay sighed. "Well, I might as well take a page out of his book now," he said, trying to find his sense of humor as he began to pull off his equipment. Jay had to admit, there was not anything funnier to him than the idea that his sister's deadbeat boyfriend would be helpful in a time like this. "I'm going to survive."

He laughed, breathing in the pressurized purity of the air sharply. Jay felt a renewed sense of calmness

ACROSS THE FLOORS OF SILENT SEAS

overtake him. He pulled off his air tank. "Yes," he said, this time even more tempted to believe the impossible. "I'm going to survive this."

Then he cheerfully tossed his air tank onto the floor behind him. The heavy canister smashed through the floor of the cave. At the sudden opening, Jay screamed, his loud cursing echoing down deep into the center of the world, gradually fading along with his consciousness.

***

He never expected to feel or sense anything ever again. But then there were murmurings and

ACROSS THE FLOORS OF SILENT SEAS

mumblings, accompanied by sounds of dripping water and hissing steam.

Jay swam slowly back to full awareness, briefly wondering if he was going to wake up in the small apartment he shared with Noelani, the one with the small walk-in closet he'd been secretly turning into a nursery for his new niece or nephew in the last few weeks. He wondered if he would open his eyes and see his headboard, or maybe the TV, since the hissing sound reminded him of the white noise that happened when he forgot to pay the cable bill.

He wondered if everything that happened to him—the swim along the floor of the ocean, the terror of being caught in a mid-shelf ridge shuffle, the mysterious orca that weirdly saved his life, and the depressing cave hidden next to the volcanic tube he'd fallen down—was somehow a dream or something.

ACROSS THE FLOORS OF SILENT SEAS

Too much drinking, maybe …

Jay's thoughts on the possibility were hopeful, but even he knew it was false hope; he never drank more than two, and even the dollar margarita nights at the Surf 'N Sun Bar and Grill were fruitless in their attempts to push him into a third drink.

The murmurings around him grew louder, and then they started to form actual words.

"What do you think it is, Paga?"

Jay felt his eyelids crackle as he tried to blink. He wanted to see who was speaking. Whoever it was, she had a lovely voice, one with a lilt that made him think of long nights and lullabies.

"I'm not sure, Sira."

Another voice this time—a voice that belonged to a man, a humble man of authority, one comfortable enough to admit his uncertainties even as he was determined to find the answers.

Her brother, boyfriend … husband, maybe? Jay wondered. Was Paga a name? It sounded familiar enough that he wondered if he had heard it before. Was it possible he had washed up on a nearby island?

His concern about location quickly eroded as his body began to trickle with pain. He felt sore and achy along his back and arms, and the cuts he had sustained earlier were screaming for medical attention. The idea that he had been having a bad dream was suddenly the silliest, stupidest idea he had ever had.

He was alive, indeed—and in terrible agony.

ACROSS THE FLOORS OF SILENT SEAS

His eyes snapped open, only to end up staring into what looked like the eyes of a stranger. Jay barely registered that he was in an open room, that he could taste the salty water in the air as he lay on a small, cold cot of sorts.

He blinked again, fully taking in the face before him. It was a humanlike face, with parts of slits running across either side of its neck; large, black eyes ringed with irises of white stared back at him. There was hair on top, long and wet and swept back before it fell in a glossy crimson wave; there were little flaps in front of where the ears were supposed to be. It was the most horrifyingly beautiful face he had ever seen.

Jay heard a long scream surround him before he realized it was coming from his own throat.

ACROSS THE FLOORS OF SILENT SEAS

"Augh!" As he realized his level of horror, he propelled himself backward.

He did not get very far. In fact, he only managed to bang his head on the wall behind him before he realized he was strapped down, lying on a medical examination slat of sorts. In addition, he learned that his body was directly against any movement at all. He moaned at only moving mere inches. He felt throbbing pain coming from the back of his head, still clothed inside the damaged hood of his wetsuit.

Paga leaned forward to examine him, a seemingly curious expression on his alien face. "Well, he's definitely awake now."

"Ouch," Jay whimpered, rubbing his head. He shoved his hands in front of his eyes, rubbing them, trying to get the clarity of his vision back.

When he opened them up again, he was still able to see the lovely creature.

He saw the other one, too—*Paga*, he thought, forcing himself to acclimate himself to his new surroundings as any proper scientist would.

He failed. He was too distracted by the lady creature. *Sira*, he remembered.

As he studied her once more, Jay silently vowed to draw her face into his mind in such detail that he would carry it until he died.

Which, he reminded himself, could be any moment.

But getting to see Sira might have made all his life worth it, he decided. She was breathtaking, now that he was too shocked to move or speak or scream. She

ACROSS THE FLOORS OF SILENT SEAS

was obviously not a human, but she was a humanoid being. Her skin had a greenish tint to it, her hands were webbed, and her legs were covered in scales. Jay had no notion of how old she actually was, but from her demeanor and the way she carried herself, she seemed close to him in age.

Her clothes were odd, he thought, but he decided it was not in a bad way. She wore a tight-fitting suit, one that reminded him of his own, but with much more style. The skintight tunic bellowed out into a short skirt of sorts, ending just below her hips. The folded material wafted gently, just as smooth as the curtain of her hair. Jay briefly thought of Noelani.

Lani would like her outfit ...

Jay did a double take, as it suddenly hit him that standing before him was a mermaid.

"Mermaid!" he gasped. "You're a mermaid."

Sira looked over at the merman beside her. "I'm not familiar with this method of communication. What do you think, Paga?"

"What's wrong with me?" Jay frowned. He could understand her. Why was she not able to understand him?

As his ears suddenly popped again, he suddenly realized the problem. Behind the protection of his hood, his lips were swollen and cracked, achingly stretched into the wetsuit material. Nothing he was saying was coming out more than a muffled shriek.

"He seems to be an intelligent animal," Paga remarked, irritating Jay enough that he tried to wriggle out of his bonds once more. The answering pain in his body only made him regret it.

"'He?'" Sira bristled. "How can you tell it's a male? It doesn't have any obvious genitals or other general sex markers."

Jay lurched forward, struggling to look down at his body, quickly giving himself a panicked examination. Realizing Sira was likely confused by his wetsuit, he nearly laughed. Because of the suit's synthetic fibers, mixed in with different sensory materials, she was unable to see his form clearly, along with the general sex characteristics she had mentioned.

As Jay sighed in relief, glad to see his manhood was present and intact, Paga and Sira continued to talk beside him.

"Perhaps it is a less-evolved form of merman," Sira suggested.

Jay's eyes went wide. *They think I'm an ape … or a fish!*

Paga shrugged. "Several tides have passed since we transported him here. We better alert the city leaders that he is awake now."

Jay glared at the merman, taking a quick study of his profile as he did his best to convey his contempt.

Paga was definitely several years older than Sira. He was pretty sure, anyway; he had always been good at guessing ages, and even though Paga was a merman, Jay was determined to keep his good record intact.

Paga had a small ruffle of a beard against his greenish cheeks, with purplish bags underneath his merman eyes. Paga looked every part the underwater sage, and Jay could not help but wonder if that somehow made him more like a human or less.

Just as Jay realized that his marine biology degree would probably be more helpful at this point, Sira crossed her arms over her chest. Jay, instinctively taking in the slightest change in all her features, almost smiled. If growing up with Noelani taught him anything, it was how to recognize a sister's moods. Looking at Sira now, he knew she was prepping for combat. Jay did not envy Paga in the least.

"I know that, Paga," Sira agreed. "Why else do you think the city elders will be interested to see it?"

"They are curious, for one. It's not every high tide that you see something fall down from the ocean," Paga said, waving toward a window.

ACROSS THE FLOORS OF SILENT SEAS

Jay followed the direction of Paga's gaze.

Instantly, he felt his jaw crack and tasted salty mist as

his mouth dropped open. From where he was lying,

Jay could see that he was not on any island at all.

Outside the window, the sky was an ocean. Rather

than an endless airway filled with wafty clouds and

clear blue coloring, there was an ocean. Mountains

and volcanoes dropped down from it like large

stalagmites, with mist and steam wafting from the

inverted horizon. It was like being in the underwater

cave all over again, he realized, with the air trapped

beneath the sea.

Under the ocean's end, Jay saw a whole

community built upon dry land. There were buildings,

many that looked like hovels, made of similar or even

the same material as the room where he found

himself. Warm steam spurt out across the area, as volcanic leaks gave forth vegetation and fire light.

It was a world not too different from his own—just one that was literally turned upside down.

As Jay stared, taking in everything with a sense of wonder and fear, he could not help but wonder if he was in hell, where he would eventually be collected by a canning company, chopped up into shredded tuna, and then eaten as some kind of grand delicacy or human sacrifice.

Paga cleared his throat behind him. "The city elders will want to make sure he is not dangerous, either."

"You should be able to tell them he's not."

"I'm only one of the leaders," Paga reminded her. "And they don't listen to me much as it is. They will want to see for themselves."

"Perhaps they will if we run some tests, now that it's awake and showing signs of sentience," Sira said. "If it is a lesser evolved form, its bionucleotides should be able to tell us quite a bit."

Jay did not like the unhealthy excitement that appeared on Sira's face. It made her look uglier, and it made him feel nervous.

"Sira, I know you're always eager to learn," Paga said patiently. "But I'm asking you, as your only brother, to wait."

"Why?" Sira scowled, drawing deep lines into her lovely face. "It's just an animal. I should be finished with the tests in a few weeks. And it's not like the city elders are really going to have any problem with me testing it."

"I know," Paga said. "But I have a feeling about this one."

Sira groaned. "Paga, we've been through this. Feelings like the ones you get don't have any basis in scientific fact."

"I'm not thinking of science, funnily enough."

Jay just stared back at them, still too confused and upset and overwhelmed to think of anything to say.

Sira put a webbed hand on her hip. "What is it then?" she asked. "I mean, there's no question it's— alright, *he's*—an animal, but still, I'm not sure that they would want to eat it before we test—"

Realizing that he might actually end up as their dinner, Jay suddenly swirled around. "I'm not an animal," he said. At the force of his words, he could finally hear just how awful his speech impediment was. His jaw locked up at the hard consonants, and his tongue felt twice as big as normal. He swirled it around, trying to find a way to speak clearly.

Sira stepped back. "Look at that! He's trying to escape his bonds. I should get some of the Patrols in here."

Before Sira could leave, Paga shook his head. "I don't think that will be necessary."

"What?" Sira shook back her long hair, frustrated. "What are you talking about?"

"Sira … I have a feeling," Paga said. "I'm wondering … well, never mind."

"What is it, Paga?"

Jay did not have to guess at the merman's hesitancy, any more than he had to guess at Sira's irritation.

"I have a feeling," Paga repeated.

"Tell me about your superstitions then, so I can tell you why you're wrong," Sira said.

"It's not that kind of feeling," Paga said. "I just meant that he's probably hungry."

At his tone, Jay had a feeling that Paga was covering for himself.

Sira seemed to miss that. Her cheeks flustered over. "That's a possibility," she agreed. "I wonder what kind of food this creature eats."

ACROSS THE FLOORS OF SILENT SEAS

Jay had wondered if Sira and Paga got along the same way he did with Noelani—making fun of each other while having fun, and then going home and bonding over video games or cooking dinner. But when Paga sighed ruefully, Jay knew for certain Sira's derision for her brother was quite real.

"I have a feeling," Paga said, his tone careful, "that this is a human."

Jay was just about to jump up and down, so happy to feel such relief that someone finally knew the truth, when Sira laughed.

She flicked her hair back over her shoulder in haughty disdain. "Paga, please. We all know that there are no such things as humans."

"Our ancestors believed in them," Paga said. "Surely their records on the matter are based on real events, Sira."

"Please, Paga, that's insane," Sira said. She tutted her slippery lips together dismissively. "Everyone knows that our ancestors did not have the advantages that we have now. What they thought was true would not hold up into today's world. They probably just saw a small, disfigured whale and called it a human."

"Stop it! He's right," Jay said, as he tried to slip his wrists out of their bonds. The pain increased before he collapsed back into the bedding. He felt angry at Sira's mocking scorn, and he was even more upset at her disbelief.

Jay was glad Paga held his ground.

"No, it's very possible he's a human," Paga insisted.

"Please, stop this. Next you'll want to talk about angels and fallen stars and life after death. You know that the rest of the community is upset with you since you tried to launch that capsule of yours during last year's High Tide."

"Please, Sira, let it go. It almost worked," Paga said. "Next time, it will be ready, and then we can see if there is a human world outside our own."

"Those who try to leave never survive, Paga, and you only encourage reckless behavior with your attempts." Sira shook her head. "Besides, what would the others say? Elona is about to give birth to your offspring. Even if your machine is 'ready' for another test flight, you would be foolish to leave her."

"You're the one who only wants to dissect this human to get data," Paga reminded her, his tone suddenly hardened.

"Hey! Hey, you!" Jay cried out again, letting words of all sorts come out, as he tried to show them Paga was right. "He's right! I'm a human!"

Sira only shook her head, coming up beside him. "Shhh, pet," she whispered tenderly. Jay was so entranced, he forgot she thought he was an animal. Her voice swept over him in lovely waves, and as her hand came down on his forehead, he found himself go still and silent. He felt a strange sort of power emanate from her, and he had to wonder if she was using magic.

Why not? Jay wondered, unable to be anything but content despite his situation. *Mermaids, magic … anything at all is possible at this point.*

"Whatever creature it is," Sira said, "it looks like it could use some medical treatment."

"I won't argue with you there," Paga said.

Over the next several moments, Sira tended to his wounds, wrapping up the cuts with kelp-like bandages, putting cold compresses on his head and his shoulders, and wiping off his wetsuit.

"This is unusual skin," she murmured. She glanced back at Paga, who had gone into a bout of thoughtful shame. "Do you think Elona will need to see him?"

ACROSS THE FLOORS OF SILENT SEAS

Jay was surprised to see Paga's eyes—all black, with white irises, the same as Sira's—crinkle with delight.

"I'm sure," Paga said. "You know Elona is always happy to help take care of the more unusual medical community needs, even when she's in the condition she's in."

Sira laughed again, making him think of Noelani. "Do you think she'll think it's a human, too?"

"Maybe," Paga replied, waving it away. "Either way, the city council leaders will want to see him soon. Why don't you go and inform them that he has woken up? I'll stay here and guard the specimen."

Jay was surprised when Sira did not argue. It seemed they had arrived at a silent truce of sorts.

Sira tossed one of the medical sponges she had been using into a disposal unit. "Sounds like a good idea," she said. She scooted around Paga's form before heading out the door behind him. "You know I love telling them good news."

As much as he was frustrated by Sira's attitude, Jay felt sad as he watched her walk out the doorway. Her scaly hips moved with the same lull as the ocean, and the outfit she wore only seemed to highlight the curves of her body.

"She's beautiful," Jay murmured, before he remembered he was just speaking gibberish, as far as the merman before him was concerned. He jiggled the straps around his wrists, wishing he would be able to take his suit's mask off his face.

Lani would be upset with me for finding her attractive. Jay smiled ruefully. Noelani, as his original wingman, would also be upset if he didn't get her phone number.

Assuming this world had phones.

Before he could wonder about Sira too much, Paga cleared his throat.

"I must apologize. Sira doesn't agree with me very often when it comes to matters that require more faith than data."

Jay turned his attention back to the merman, watching as he leaned against the smooth wall behind him. Despite his education as a scientist, Jay was surprised to notice Paga shared some of the same features as Sira. He had the same thoughtful lines on his face, the same intelligent gleam in his eye. But

ACROSS THE FLOORS OF SILENT SEAS

there was also more compassion there, too, and Jay was suddenly relieved to find that empathy was more universal than he'd originally thought.

Paga stepped forward and unlocked one of Jay's arms. "Give me your hand," he said, reaching out his own webbed hand.

Jay did not hesitate; it was the perfect chance to show the merman that he could understand his speech. He inched out with his hand, unable to stop wondering if his aching cuts and scrapes on it would hurt at the contact.

But the moment his fingers wrapped around the merman's webbed palm, Jay felt an unusual sensation take ahold of him.

Light flashed, and Jay saw his own life pass before his eyes.

ACROSS THE FLOORS OF SILENT SEAS

He saw himself as a young boy, as he stood between his abusive, drunk-as-a-fish father and Noelani; he watched his teenage self go sailing for the first time, riding on the speedboat he'd stolen from his hometown marina, looking for the solace only the ocean could ever seem to offer to him; he watched Noelani bail him out of jail, before he saw her getting his dorm room set up at UC.

Jay felt his mouth drop open as he suddenly saw Noelani on the *Pedro*. She was wearing the same outfit he had last seen her in, the black tube top with the red Hawaiian print pants. Any other time, he would have smiled, seeing her self-assured style. But he was too shocked to realize that he was watching her as she called for him.

"Jay!" Noelani cried out as she stood in front of a monitor, hitting the sonar equipment in anger and

ACROSS THE FLOORS OF SILENT SEAS

despair. When she fell down to the deck, slumping over in a fit of tears, Kekoa came up behind her, obviously trying to comfort her despite the hindrance of his injured wrist. Jay was floored, realizing that he could see her without having seen her.

He watched, terrified, as she grabbed her pregnant belly and began crying hard.

"Lani," Jay murmured, as the vision faded and the underwater world before him resurfaced along with his despair.

His eyes, still wide, turned back to Paga.

"So," Paga remarked, rubbing his one hand over his chin. "You *are* a human."

Jay nodded.

"We've heard of humans down here," Paga said. "But most of the stories we have are the ones we tell our children."

Jay nodded again.

"When I saw you react to Sira's comments, I had a feeling you were from the upper world," Paga continued. "Humans are supposed to be able to learn languages much more easily than other animals."

Jay looked down at Paga's hand. If he were not already overwhelmed with surprises, he would have been more shocked to see that it was glowing.

"That's my special power, as a city elder," Paga explained. The glowing stopped a second later. "It's a special power that's passed down through the different generations, leading all the way back to Rasulka's original city founders."

Jay nodded again, hoping he would be able to figure out more ways to communicate with Paga.

Maybe he will be able to help me get back to Lani.

There was a rustle outside the room, and Paga looked back at him. "You've been injured quite badly," he said. His mouth quirked up into a small smile. "If you couldn't tell, I mean."

Jay nodded, but he was starting to get irritated at the merman. *How is this helping me?* Jay wondered.

"I'm going to tell you this now," Paga said. "The city elders do not believe in humans. If they do think you are a human, they will likely kill you. And even if they don't, they could shut you away in our city palace, and you will never be able to return to your family."

Jay perked up at the thought of getting back home, but Paga's warning sank through him, torpedoing the last of his hope.

At his reaction, Paga reached forward and rested his webbed hand on Jay's arm. "I'll take that to mean that you want to get back home. If you do, I will need your help. And you must trust me. Do you understand?"

Jay nearly wept, as a surge of hope sparked once more inside of him. He could see himself back home already, sharing his story of his adventures with Noelani's baby. Noelani would be ecstatic to learn there were such things as mermaids, and they lived underneath the ocean and used it as their sky.

And her reaction would be nothing compared to the university's. Jay suddenly wondered if he could get a book deal big enough to pay off all his student loans.

Paga sighed. "Well, that's that. Before we can do anything, we must see about getting your injuries taken care of. Sira has some power to help you, but you will not be able to count on her to help us get you back home."

Jay thought about how he had felt when Sira touched his forehead. *Healing powers? Calming powers?*

He was just trying to remember that exact feeling when he felt his whole body go numb. He gazed sleepily over at Paga, who was pressing some buttons by his cot.

"I hope you will forgive me," Paga said. "But I know that the healing process can be sped up by sleep. And it is really for the best that you are asleep when the city elders get here."

Jay felt the world around him start to disappear once more, as he slowly fell back to sleep. He silently said another quick prayer, hoping beyond hope that God was done teasing him and that he would not only wake up again, but that he would soon be safely home.

***

Long days or even weeks later—it was hard to estimate—Jay found his body working to repair itself, despite the efforts of the merfolk coming and going in what he assumed was their hospital.

Paga and Sira, and other merfolk, wandered in throughout his brief periods of waking. Some of them made comments; some of them took samples of all kinds from him. There were some instances when he would scream and others where he would cry. When they finally allowed him to have his hands freed, Jay reveled in Sira's shocked expression as he peeled the hooded mask of his wetsuit from his face.

"Stop poking me!" he yelled, further surprising her with his first clear words in what felt like—and probably was—several days.

Sira's mouth dropped open, but she quickly recovered. "Well," Sira exclaimed, "that sure explains a lot! You just needed to shed your outer skin."

He frowned at her. "It's not skin."

ACROSS THE FLOORS OF SILENT SEAS

"Is it an exoskeleton?" she asked, starting to tug at the wetsuit, seeing if she could pull it off him. She tore off a small patch and examined closely, her black irises going wide. "Hmm … it feels like skin, but it is too fine."

At her touch, Jay swallowed hard. He was suddenly very conscious of his nearly naked, putrid-smelling body, covered only in his suit and a thin undergarment. If it were not for all the hissing machines hooked up to him, Jay wondered if he would be even more repugnant. There was a grimy, unbelievably salty taste in his mouth, after a still unknown length of time down in Rasulka.

"What's wrong?" Sira asked, noticing his duress.

Jay blushed. He felt unprepared for her scientific scrutiny in that regard, especially since, despite her often pretentious observations and silly questions, he actually liked Sira.

She was curious and rational, and her tendency to talk aloud, even when she ended up insulting him, shed a lot of light on who she was, what her job was, and where he was. That was how he knew that he was living in a city-state known as Rusalka, and they were governed by the eight city elders, two of whom were Paga and Sira. Jay had met some of the other ones, and his reaction to them ranged from sympathy to anger to irritation, with only one, a merman named Ceros, making him feel absolute hatred. But as he was Sira's husband, Jay had a feeling it had more to do with that than anything else did.

As he looked at Sira, watching her gape in wonder at his lack of gills and the loosened cloth of his wetsuit, Jay felt a desperate rush of homesickness.

ACROSS THE FLOORS OF SILENT SEAS

"No," he answered. "It's not an exoskeleton. It's a wetsuit."

"Wetsuit?" Sira frowned at the strange word. "What is it for?"

"It's for underwater exploration," he clarified.

"Underwater?"

"Uh, good point. Maybe it would be overwater exploration here?" Jay laughed at the strange phrase and his own cleverness, even though Sira did not seem to understand.

He was not even sure she was trying to, since she had an angry look on her face. "No wonder my brother thinks you're a human," she said.

"I am," Jay told her. "My name is Jay."

He was hoping she would be happy to know who he was, at last. But when Sira scoffed, he felt something was wrong—just like the time before, as he was diving near the Juan de Fuca fault line.

"I know you can speak our language now," Sira said, pulling him away from his worry. "But that hardly makes you one of us. You're lucky we consider you an intelligent being at all, you know."

"I'm not one of you," Jay said, surprised to see that she was starting to get mad. "I'm a human, and an intelligent, sentient creature at that. You can see I'm not a merman."

"But you can't be a human," Sira insisted. "It's just an idea that my brother's planted in your head. Humans don't exist."

"Why do you think they don't?" Jay asked. "Even though I'm right here in front of you?"

"They just don't," Sira said. "And they can't. That would give credence to the old legends that talk about how there's a whole world above us, when that's clearly not the case."

"There is a whole world up there. I live there." Jay's heart ached again. "My family is up there."

Sira's features lost their purity as she scowled. "Just stop it," she said. "I know you've been talking to my brother about this. I know how he is."

"What do you mean?"

Sira rolled her eyes. "He told me once that he had a dream about humans," she said. "It's nonsense."

"If his dream was really just nonsense, then it shouldn't matter if I'm human," Jay argued.

Sira stepped closer to him, leaning over him menacingly. "You should really drop the topic," she said. "If we feel like you're a threat to our research, or even to our way of life, the city council will kill you. No questions or qualms about it."

"You would really kill me?" Jay was surprised how hurt he was by her callous statement. "Even after all this time you've watched over me and cared for me?"

"Of course," Sira said. "You're just an animal, really. Maybe a new species, maybe a new mutation, but still—"

"My DNA shows I'm a human," Jay insisted.

ACROSS THE FLOORS OF SILENT SEAS

"Your test results are officially marked as inconclusive!" Sira glared at him. "Nearly all of the people here agree there is no way you can be human, so you should stop this nonsense at once."

"I'm just trying to tell you the truth," Jay said.

"Ha!" Sira scoffed. "What is truth? Truth is only what you can see and observe, and you'd be a fool to believe otherwise. The truth is also that Paga has been in here more often than he should be, and the other elders of the community have noticed. Anything he has taught you to repeat will be ignored at best, and considered compromised observations at worst."

"Your logic doesn't make any sense, though. You can see me, and you should be able see that I am real. And even the things you can't see about me, like my thoughts or feelings or even my pain, that's no matter

ACROSS THE FLOORS OF SILENT SEAS

when it comes to proof. There are plenty of things you can't see that are real," Jay argued. "Some of them—love, beauty, ideas—make life worth living."

Sira crossed her arms. "Then what does it really matter if you live or die, in the end? There is just life, and death, and nothing between. We can study you just fine when you're dead."

From the way she said it, Jay suddenly had a lot more sympathy for the animals he had dissected in many of his biology classes. But he was also angry. How could Sira deny his words? His own testimony about himself? She could see for herself what he was.

"Is there any way at all," Jay asked her, "that I could get you to see that I am a human being?"

Sira's anger suddenly boiled over. "No," she said. "No, because humans do not exist. No one alive here has ever seen one, and they are nothing but fairy tales and child's play. Who would want to believe in humans anyway? All humans do is breathe in dry air and walk along roads of rocks and stones while they reproduce, all while strange, feathered fish with wings fly around out of the water. Humans are supposed to cause all sorts of problems, too, aren't they? They supposedly converse with angels and demons, but they can't seem to understand the balance of power overlapping their own mythological worlds."

"You're conversing with a human right now," Jay pointed out. "Yet you don't seem to realize that my world is real, and it has its own special power, too."

"Oh, really?" Sira scoffed. "What power is that?"

Jay floundered here, unable to put into words what was special about being a human, living in a human world.

There was something special about humanity, and he was never more certain about that as he was when Sira dismissed it. There was something that he could not explain, or at least something he suddenly wished he could explain that would make sense to Sira. For all he had known her in the time he had been there, she had sneered at the thought of life's fragility, of human beings and their existence.

He thought about how wonderfully made he was, how his body was designed, how every feature had purpose and beauty, a beauty capable of being both efficient and effervescent, how there were so many things Sira was overlooking due to superstition and willful ignorance.

ACROSS THE FLOORS OF SILENT SEAS

"See?" Sira scoffed, taking his overwhelming wonder to mean she had won the argument. She reached over and typed a code into one of his vitality monitors.

The monitor let out a soft beep. A powerful urge to fall asleep fell over him, but seeing the look on Sira's face, Jay was afraid that if he did, he would not wake up ever again.

"Are you going to kill me?" Jay murmured, his voice already more slurred with sleepiness.

"Eventually," Sira said. "Probably. If you tell me the truth, I'll likely keep you alive longer. But if you're already too corrupted by Paga and his stories, I'll be happy to continue my research with you as a chilled animal slab."

Jay was about to ask her why she thought he was lying again when a new voice cried out.

"Sira! Sira, what do you think you're doing?"

Jay breathed a sigh of relief. "Paga!"

Paga hurried forward and stopped the flow of medication into Jay's body. "That's enough," Paga said. "You might kill him."

"Our research might benefit more if he is dead," Sira insisted.

"Sira, you must stop this," Paga said.

"Me?" Sira huffed indignantly. "You're the one who taught the creature to tell us he's human!"

"He talked? And you understood him?" Paga glanced down at Jay, who nodded. He imagined that he looked quite different now, especially with his hair and his full face exposed. Jay watched as the different emotions glimmered in Paga's eyes, moving from astonishment to joy, from fear to determination.

"It's better that I introduce myself if I can, right?" Jay asked. "I'm Jay Bishop. That's my name."

After a long moment, Paga answered him. "You can talk much more clearly now, Jay Bishop."

"No," Jay said. "It's just Jay."

"Just Jay?"

"No." Jay laughed. "Jay."

"Jay." His name sounded unusual, coming from the older merman, but Jay was just happy that they were able to get it right after his time in the medical ward.

"I took off my wetsuit," Jay replied, pointing to his now-bare face.

"I see. What did you say to Sira just before I came here, Jay?" Paga asked, his voice patient.

"I told her the truth," Jay muttered, suddenly recalling Paga's earlier warning. He felt guilt tug at him, even though his pride pushed him into adding, "I told her that I'm a human being."

Paga only nodded. "We will have to consider the matter later," he said. "Sira, I came to get you. Elona would like your help. The baby is coming."

Sira hissed at him, angry and disappointed. "Fine," she snapped, storming out the door. "But this isn't over, Paga. I'm warning you. If he continues to impede my research—research ordered by the city elders, no less—I will kill him to get my answers."

ACROSS THE FLOORS OF SILENT SEAS

"I'll see what I can do," Paga promised.

Sira whirled around angrily. "You'd better. If you weren't my brother, I would try to expel you from the council, you know."

"I know that well."

"Come on, Paga. Your stories are just that— stories!"

"We'll talk about it later, Sira. Please, go and help tend to my wife. She is calling for you."

Sira groaned. "Fine!"

Paga sighed as the door shut behind her. "We must be grateful that Elona went into labor today."

"Elona?" Jay asked.

"My wife," he explained. "She is about to have our first child."

Jay softened. "My sister was going to have a baby, too."

"Going to?"

"Oh, I guess she's still going to have it," Jay said. "Or maybe she already did. I don't really know how long I've been here."

"You have been here for nearly twenty tides, but that is long enough that Sira has collected quite a bit of information from you," Paga said. "I'm glad you can talk with me now, but you must realize she is dangerously upset."

"I can see that pretty clearly."

ACROSS THE FLOORS OF SILENT SEAS

"Then, if you are truly a human, if you are what you say you are, you must know that we need to get you out of here, and soon," Paga said. "I know now that I was right before. You are the human who was destined to come down here, and others will follow you. And then our world as we know it will be over."

"What? What do you mean?" Jay felt the blood drain from his face.

"I told Sira a long time ago, when we were both elders—before our parents died, and we took their places on the council with the other city elders—that a human would appear in our world. She was angry with me then."

"Why?" Jay asked. "I mean, it doesn't sound that bad, a human coming here. I haven't been that bad of a guest, have I?"

Paga gave him a tepid smile. "After the humans appeared, I saw that our community would be destroyed."

Jay floundered for the right words to say. "I promise, I wouldn't harm anyone. Right now, I just want to go home. Lani's all alone without me. My sister," he added quickly, seeing the inquisitive look on Paga's face.

Paga nodded. "I see."

"Lani's about to have her baby, and the father doesn't seem like he'll really step up," Jay continued. "I want to be there for her. Lani's always been my whole family. Even if the father doesn't want anything to do with his baby, I want more of a family for *me*."

ACROSS THE FLOORS OF SILENT SEAS

"I understand this instinct, and I commend you for your honor." Paga took his hand. "So I will swear to you, Jay Bishop, I will do everything that I can to get you back to your family."

"Why?" Jay cocked his head thoughtfully. "Why do you want to help me? Sira is okay with killing me. Why don't you want to?"

Paga was silent for a long moment, before he let out a long, slow breath. "In my vision," he started, "I saw that I would meet a human. One who looks a lot like you, with black hair and skin with no scales. I knew that he would help us, and that I am supposed to help him."

"So your dream told you to help me?" Jay asked. He did not know whether or not to be thankful for

ACROSS THE FLOORS OF SILENT SEAS

the merman's response. "And that's why Sira is upset with you?"

Paga shrugged. "Sira does not believe that our world is governed by anything other than things she can see," he said softly. "I have always believed in something greater. Since I was a boy, I have had visions, along with the ability to read other's memories."

"Your special power is to see into other people's memories?" Jay asked. "And the future?"

Paga gave him a small smile. "I like to think the visions I get are part of the Creator's memories," he said quietly.

"You mean, like God?" Jay asked.

"God?"

Jay tried to explain who and what God was, shamefully stumbling over his many years of apathy and ignorance despite his frequent prayer for deliverance and safety. Finally, Paga frowned. "I must know him by another name," he said.

The sound of marching steps, taken in matching movements, suddenly sounded from outside his window.

Paga hurried over. "It's the city elders. They're coming, and they look angry," he said. "I feel we must leave now, if we are to keep you safe."

He released the rest of Jay's bonds, and then he hauled him to his feet. Jay felt his legs wobble dangerously, and Paga leaned down to support him.

"Thank you," Jay said. "I don't know how to repay you for all your help."

"Don't worry about it." Paga shrugged. "Besides, it might not work."

Jay watched the merman's face carefully. While Paga brought up a good point, Jay had to wonder what would happen to his rescuer if he did succeed in getting away.

Before Jay could ask, he stepped outside of the hospital and immediately started choking. The air was so full of humidity, it was like walking through a waterfall. He placed his free hand over his mouth.

"Try not to make any noise," Paga whispered as he pulled Jay around the far side of the building. Together, they hurried through the streets.

Even though he struggled to breathe properly, Jay took the time to get a good look around the place of his captivity.

ACROSS THE FLOORS OF SILENT SEAS

He immediately wished he had eight more eyes and several more days to explore the strange city of Rasulka. While most of the buildings were made with domed tops and rounded walls, there were colors of all kind that decorated them. Windows were carved into the buildings, reminding Jay of gothic buildings and ancient palaces.

He knew their reliance on technology was as real as it was in his own world. There were ceramic-like structures that whirred with noise, and glassy equipment that glittered in the hands of the native merfolk.

This is a beautiful place, Jay thought. *It's just not my home.*

"—and that's why I've been experimenting with my design."

Paga's words cut through Jay's hazy delight. Jay reminded himself that he should be concentrating on what Paga was saying. But as he twisted his way toward the city outskirts, still in awe at the sights before him, Jay barely heard the merman talk about his machine, how it had been given to him in another vision, how he wasn't sure if it was ready to go, but that they had no other options left.

"Are you able to do this?"

"Huh?" Jay whipped his head back around to face Paga. "What did you say?"

"I asked if you are sure you are able to go through with this," Paga repeated patiently, even though he was clearly irked Jay had not been paying attention. "There's no guarantee that you'll live."

All the awe and delight flushed out of him. Was he willing to die in order to gain the chance to leave?

No, I'm not, Jay thought. *But I am willing to risk dying if it means seeing Lani again.*

He had worked all his life to take care of his sister, despite all the difficulties. Facing death, and fighting for his freedom, would not prove to be an exception now.

"I have no choice," Jay said slowly, as he faced Paga. "Lani needs me. And they'll kill me if I stay here, won't they?"

"Most likely, especially since I have helped you run away," Paga agreed. "But there's still a chance they won't. Sira is angry with you, and horrified by the idea of humans, but she is only one member of the council. I still might be able to sway them to provide you with a better fate down here in Rasulka."

But what fate would that be? Jay didn't have to think very long before he saw himself living as a glorified zoo animal, on display at a museum, or left to be killed as part of the process of scientific discovery.

And what about Paga? He likely would not be able to convince the city elders to do anything, especially since he had already helped him escape Sira's wrath.

"You've already gotten me out of the hospital," Jay said. "It's too late to turn back now."

"Hospital?" Paga looked confused, before he laughed. "Oh, you mean the research lab."

Jay felt the blood drain from his face.

The rest of the journey to Paga's house beyond the heart of Rasulka was uneventful, if longer than expected. He was surprised to see the merman's hovel; as a city elder, he expected something larger and more grand in scale.

"I'm the council's longest-serving member," Paga explained. "As such, I can have any house I want. I chose this one."

"Why?" Jay asked incredulously, thinking of some of the tall and luxurious hovels he had seen on the way here.

"Elona likes her privacy, for one. For another, the high mountain provides a lovely view. And," he added slyly, "it also provides a lot of cover for me to work."

Jay suddenly heard shouts crying out from the city behind them, and he felt an urgent need to flee. "I'm ready to go," he said.

"Good. This way."

Paga assisted Jay around his home and headed into the rocky shelf.

Jay tried not to whimper, as he limped through the jagged passages, wincing as stones cut into his feet, still half-covered with his soppy, ripped suit.

He did not think it was possible, but Jay felt much worse when he saw the so-called machine Paga had been building.

"This is it," Paga said, and Jay's heart did another flip.

The machine itself looked like a space capsule, Jay decided. It had a circular windshield of sorts, attached to a long, tubular body. The glass looked thick and the capsule sturdy, and it almost reminded Jay of one of the old submarines that UC had in its catalogue of underwater diving vehicles.

Still, Jay wondered for a long moment if his bodily pain had begun to affect his logic.

But then he rejected it. He had survived growing up with his abusive father, and protecting Noelani from all sorts of harm. He could do this. He could climb into the strange pod and risk his life trying to get back to the top of the world. He would do it for her, and her baby, if nothing else.

"Well, what do you think?" Paga asked. "It's beautiful, isn't it?"

ACROSS THE FLOORS OF SILENT SEAS

Jay did not want to tell Paga that it looked like something a sixth-grade science class would put together with scraps and spare garbage.

The sounds of the city folk rising against him saved him from responding.

Jay cocked his head back toward the yelling. "I think it's time to go," he said, resigning himself to his fate.

Paga nodded. "Excellent."

If Paga believed in something greater, Jay thought, he could, too. He had found out mermaids were real, right?

Who is to say that miracles aren't as well?

He thought he had largely given up on faith. But now, faced with death, Jay was ready to take the most unexpected leap of faith in his entire life.

Still, Jay tried not to think about dying while Paga strapped him inside the small cockpit seat.

Paga held out his hand. "Here," he said. "Take it."

Jay frowned, but he reached out and took the merman's hand once more.

Immediately, a new vision swam into his mind.

There was Noelani, with a baby in her arms, one with a little tuft of hair above his scrunched-up face. Jay felt his eyes water, but not before he saw himself—a shaky, thin shadow of his former self— approach her, holding out his arms.

ACROSS THE FLOORS OF SILENT SEAS

"That's your nephew," Paga told him quietly, as the vision faded. "He's a good kid. Your sister, Lani, was it? She named him Milo."

"That's my middle name," Jay whispered, finding it hard to swallow all of a sudden.

"If he's anything like you," Paga said, "I'll look forward to meeting him one day."

Jay barely heard Paga give him last-second instructions on how to steer, how to eject, and so on and so forth. All he could think about was that tiny baby.

His tiny baby nephew.

I'm going to live, Jay realized, with a profound sense of the miraculous. He felt grateful tears finally fall free

ACROSS THE FLOORS OF SILENT SEAS

as the machine roared to life, and Paga waved goodbye.

The pressure of flight hit Jay hard as the capsule launched, piercing the watery skies of Rasulka. He felt the weight of the underwater world all around him, but his heart was flying free as the hours passed.

Throughout his trip, Jay allowed himself to alternatively pass into sleep awareness and waking wonder.

He no longer wondered if he was going to die but he began to fear it less. He had witnessed so much the world had yet to see.

Gradually, the darkness of the ocean, deep inside the heart of the earth, faded with the sudden sight of muffled light.

He had made it to the other side. He had made it back.

There was a swift movement beside him. Jay glanced over to see there was a whale swimming beside him, almost as though he was escorting him back home.

Home.

He thought of that vision again, the one Paga had given him; Jay thought of his sister and her son. He thought of how much more he wanted that now, how close he had been to losing it.

And then he looked around, looking around the small cabin of his capsule, gazing past the orca to watch as he passed through the world he loved best.

No, he thought. *Not best. Not anymore.*

ACROSS THE FLOORS OF SILENT SEAS

Jay felt a laugh swell up inside of him. He wondered what Noelani's expression would be, when he reunited with her; he wondered how Milo would react, in meeting him for the first time; he wondered if Dr. Marley or the university would believe him or not.

Dr. Marley? That's a big maybe. But the university? No way.

He sighed, thinking of Sira again. Jay had to admit, he did not know if he wanted to tell anyone at the school about her anyway. Her face was beautiful, but there was too much of an unnamed ugliness deep within her. He was not able to separate those truths from reality, and he found he could not think of one without thinking of the other.

After a few more moments, Jay let her go. He let the memory of Sira's face fall away with the shadows of the silent sea. He had someone else to love, someone who made his life more beautiful, and without any effort.

"I'm coming home, Milo," he whispered. "I'm coming home to you. And boy, do I have a story to tell you when I get there."

C. S. JOHNSON

97

ACROSS THE FLOORS OF SILENT SEAS

C. S. Johnson is the author of several young adult novels, including sci-fi and fantasy adventures such as *The Starlight Chronicles* series, the *Once Upon a Princess* saga, and the *Divine Space Pirates* trilogy. With a gift for sarcasm and an apologetic heart, she currently lives in Atlanta with her family.

ACROSS THE FLOORS OF SILENT SEAS

C. S. JOHNSON

99

ACROSS THE FLOORS OF SILENT SEAS

THANK YOU FOR PICKING UP THIS BOOK!

To Get *Awakening* (A Special Christmas Episode of
The *Starlight Chronicles*) for Free,
Click Here

Download It At:
https://www.csjohnson.me/awakening

ACROSS THE FLOORS OF SILENT SEAS

ACROSS THE FLOORS OF SILENT SEAS

AUTHOR'S NOTE

Dear Reader,

Thank you once more for picking up this portal and delving into a new world of mine. *Across the Floors of Silent Seas* is a prequel to my upcoming novel *Till Human Voices Wake Us*, and both of them deal with some of the same questions that have been amusing me as I planned out the books, starting with the most obvious one: "Do Mermaids believe in Humans?"

The follow-up question is a dangerous one: "What if … ?"

What if there was a mermaid community living under Hollywood and Southern California? What if they believed that humans were myths and nice stories for children, the way people believe in ghosts and angels up here? What would happen if a human found his way down there—and what if his way down was not actually an accident, but a matter of destiny?

I thought those questions were intriguing enough to consider for the story, but I further hope this story inspires you to consider other possibilities. In many ways, this story is a small (very small) tribute to Jesus of Nazareth. He came to a world where they did not believe in him when he told them who he was, and even those who were looking for him did not seem to know much about him or his plans. I have seen so many "sympathize with the bad guy" tropes in recent media—not all bad stories, and not a bad route to consider for character—but I feel like too many stories can allow us to forget our sympathies should not impede us from pursuing true truth and justice. I also feel it is to our benefit to remind ourselves that our sympathies, dangerously misplaced, easily allow us to cast the hero into the role of the villain.

Thank you for your time in reading my work! I hope I have given you something to think about while I work on the novel companion to this piece, *Till Human Voices Wake Us*, where you will not only get to meet Jay again, but also his nephew, Milo, and Paga's daughter, Eluia, as fate finds a way for them to once more resume their undersea adventures together.

Until We Meet Again,

C. S. Johnson

AUTHOR'S ACKNOWLEDGEMENTS

EDITOR

Jennifer C. Sell

Jennifer Clark Sell is a professional book editor and proofreader. She works from her home in Southern California. With her years of professional and personal experience, she offers several quality packages for authors.

Find her at https://www.facebook.com/JenniferSellEditingService.

Photo Credit: Savannah Sell

105

ACROSS THE FLOORS OF SILENT SEAS

OTHER WORKS BY THE AUTHOR

The Starlight Chronicles, by C. S. Johnson

Everyone has a set of beliefs that sets them apart from others.

When a meteorite strikes the heart of Apollo City, sixteen-year-old Hamilton Dinger finds all of his beliefs—mainly in himself—unable to stand against the reality of his supernatural powers. Tensions increase as the meteorite unlocks the Seven Deadly Sinisters, and their leader, Orpheus, and they begin to attack the city's citizens. With Elysian, a changeling dragon, and Starry Knight, a beautiful but dangerous warrior, Hamilton must overcome his inner struggles, seal away the bad guys, and still finish his homework. Join Hamilton throughout this seven-book series as he becomes the superhero Wingdinger and sets out to save the day … and the world.

Once Upon a Princess, by C. S. Johnson

Life is unfair, even for princesses.

When Rose—officially Princess Aurora Rosemarie— was born, she was cursed by Magdalina, the wicked rulers of the fairies. Under her curse, Rose is destined to prick her finger and die on her eighteenth birthday.

When Rose learns of her curse, she sets out to do what she can to break it. Along for the ride are her friends Theo, raised in the church, but in search of his own vengeance; Mary, a young fairy who has watched over Rose since she was little; and Ethan and Sophia, a pair of siblings with a troubled past.

Can Rose find a way to break her curse and save herself? Find out in this four-part novella series, inspired by *Sleeping Beauty*.

The Divine Space Pirates, by C. S. Johnson

If survival is all that matters, does truth still make a difference?

There is nothing Aerie St. Cloud wants more than her family unit's love—until she is accidentally captured by the fearsome space pirate, Captain Chainsword, and she is stuck on his pirated starship, the *Perdition*. Aerie soon realizes the difference that the truth does make, as she finds herself falling in love with the tragic space pirate captain. Can her love help bridge the gap between her worlds? Or will it just lead to more destruction?

ACROSS THE FLOORS OF SILENT SEAS

Thank you for reading! Please leave a review for this book and check for other books and updates!

C. S. JOHNSON

ACROSS THE FLOORS OF SILENT SEAS

ACROSS THE FLOORS OF SILENT SEAS